Level 8 – Purple

Helpful Hints for Reading at Home

The graphemes (written letters) and phonemes (units of sound) used throughout this series are aligned with Letters and Sounds. This offers a consistent approach to learning whether reading at home or in the classroom. Books levelled as 'a' are an introduction to this band. Readers can advance to 'b' where graphemes are consolidated and further graphemes are introduced.

HERE IS A LIST OF ALTERNATIVE GRAPHEMES FOR THIS PHASE OF LEARNING. AN EXAMPLE OF THE PRONUNCIATION CAN BE FOUND IN BRACKETS.

Phase 5 Alternative Pronunciations of Graphemes			
a (hat, what)	e (bed, she)	i (fin, find)	o (hot, so)
u (but, unit)	c (cat, cent)	g (got, giant)	ow (cow, blow)
ie (tied, field)	ea (eat, bread)	er (farmer, herb)	ch (chin, school, chef)
y (yes, by, very)	ou (out, shoulder, could, you)		
o_e (home)	u_e (rule)		

HERE ARE SOME WORDS WHICH YOUR CHILD MAY FIND TRICKY.

Phase 5 Tricky Words			
oh	their	people	Mr
Mrs	looked	called	asked
could			

TOP TIPS FOR HELPING YOUR CHILD TO READ:

- Allow children time to break down unfamiliar words into units of sound and then encourage children to string these sounds together to create the word.
- Encourage your child to point out any focus phonics when they are used.
- Read through the book more than once to grow confidence.
- Ask simple questions about the text to assess understanding.
- Encourage children to use illustrations as prompts.

This book is a 'b' level and is a purple level 8 book band.

The Smell That Wasn't Funny

Written by
John Wood

Illustrated by
Simona Hodonova

There were four clowns in a small car.
Their names were Pete, Bibs, Whitman and Teeny. It was their day off and they were going to the theme park.

They were all being funny.
"Me next! I'm going to tell a joke," said Bibs.
"What do you call a – "

Suddenly, Whitman shrieked.
"What is that smell?" he yelled. "It is awful!"
Pete looked like he was going to be sick.
Bibs couldn't believe how bad it smelled.

The smell was so bad that Whitman's eyes filled with tears. He couldn't see, and the car swerved to the left. They were heading for the huge chasm.

"Stop!" shouted Teeny.

Whitman stamped on the brakes. The wheels screeched and the car quickly came to a standstill.

"Quick! Get out!" said Bibs, scrabbling to get out of the car.

The clowns ran outside, as far away from the car as they could. Whitman looked at the others.

"Who made that smell?" he said.

He was very angry.

"It was Pete," said Bibs. He pointed with a shaky finger. "There was a sound that came from his bum. It sounded like parp."

"That wasn't me!" shouted Pete. "I sat on my horn by accident."
Pete pulled out a small horn from his pocket.
He gave it a squeeze.
Parp, went the horn.

Whitman snatched the horn from Pete.
"Well, where did the smell come from then?" asked Whitman. "Was it something in the car?"
The clowns groaned. They didn't want to go back to the car but they had to.

The clowns held their breath. They dashed to the car, and tried to find what had made the awful, awful smell.

There was a lot of stuff in the car to sort out. Teeny threw out a trapeze. Whitman threw out a bike with one wheel.

The clowns were running out of air. They sorted even quicker. Bibs threw out some food that Teeny used for juggling. There were potatoes, lettuces and swedes.

"Oh yuck!" groaned Pete, jumping up and down. He had found something. It was an old bag of Chinese food. Nobody knew how long it had been under the seats.

Pete sniffed the Chinese food. It did not smell good. But the Chinese food hadn't made the bad smell. Pete threw it back under the seat.

The clowns ran back to safety. They were panting and wheezing. Whitman kicked a stone in anger.

"It was one of you! I know it!" he yelled.

"Stop it, Whitman," said Pete. "You are making a scene."
"I don't care if I am making a scene," shouted Whitman. He threw a pie at Pete, but it whizzed past his head.

Pete and Whitman started fighting. Bibs sat down and put his head in his hands. They were never going to get to the theme park now.

"Today has been awful," said Bibs, sadly. Suddenly Pete and Whitman fell into the chasm! Teeny and Bibs gasped and jumped after them.

The clowns cartwheeled down the slope. They went faster and faster until...

WHACK!

The clowns landed on each other. They were so dazed that they didn't know where they were. Suddenly Pete and Whitman remembered that they were meant to be fighting.

Pete whipped out a water gun. Whitman took out a water balloon.

"Stop!" said Teeny for the second time that day. "Let's not fight!"

"Remember, what is the most important rule
for clowns?" asked Teeny.
"Don't juggle eggs!" said Bibs, proudly.
"No, he means the other rule," said Whitman.
"Always stick together."
The clowns hugged each other.

Soon it was evening. The clowns didn't know how to get back to the car, so they found a place to lie down.

"What if animals come in the night?" whispered Teeny. "Or thieves?"

"Or white tigers with big whiskers," whispered Bibs.
"I'll keep you safe," said Whitman.
The Sun went down. The clowns stayed together to keep warm.

In the sky, the stars appeared, one by one.
Suddenly a parp echoed in the dark.
"Whoops! I must have sat on my horn again,"
said Pete.

"But Pete, I still have your horn," said Whitman. The clowns looked at each other in fear. Then they sniffed an awful whiff. The smell was back!

The Smell that Wasn't Funny

1. Where were the clowns going on their day off?

2. What did the clowns find under the seats in the car?

   (a) A water balloon

   (b) A horn

   (c) An old bag of Chinese food

3. Why do you think Pete and Whitman were fighting?

4. What is the most important rule for clowns?

5. What do you think the awful smell was? Do you think Pete should have admitted it was him all along?

King's Lynn, Norfolk PE30 4LS

ISBN 978-1-83927-313-1

 Printed in Malaysia.
A catalogue record for this book is available from the British Library.

The Smell that Wasn't Funny
Written by John Wood
Illustrated by Simona Hodonova

An Introduction to BookLife Readers...

Our Readers have been specifically created in line with the London Institute of Education's approach to book banding and are phonetically decodable and ordered to support each phase of the Letters and Sounds document.

Each book has been created to provide the best possible reading and learning experience. Our aim is to share our love of books with children, providing both emerging readers and prolific page-turners with beautiful books that are guaranteed to provoke interest and learning, regardless of ability.

BOOK BAND GRADED using the Institute of Education's approach to levelling.

PHONETICALLY DECODABLE supporting each phase of Letters and Sounds.

EXERCISES AND QUESTIONS to offer reinforcement and to ascertain comprehension.

BEAUTIFULLY ILLUSTRATED to inspire and provoke engagement, providing a variety of styles for the reader to enjoy whilst reading through the series.

AUTHOR INSIGHT:
JOHN WOOD

An incredibly creative and talented author, John Wood has written about 60 books for BookLife Publishing. Born in Warwickshire, he graduated with a BA in English Literature and English Language from De Montford University. During his studies, he learned about literature, styles of language, linguistic relativism, and psycholinguistics, which is the study of the effects of language on the brain. Thanks to his learnings, John successfully uses words that captivate and resonate with children and that will be sure to make them retain information. His stories are entertaining, memorable, and extremely fun to read.

This book is a 'b' level and is a purple level 8 book band.